The Owl
and the
Pussy-cat

Edward Lear

Illustrated by Victoria Ball

The Owl and the Pussy-cat
went to sea
in a beautiful
pea-green boat.

They took some honey,
and plenty of money,
wrapped up in a
five-pound note.

The Owl looked up
to the stars above,
and sang to a small guitar.

"O lovely Pussy! O Pussy, my love,
What a beautiful Pussy you are, you are, you are!

What a beautiful
Pussy you are."

Pussy said to the Owl,
"You elegant fowl,

"Oh let us be married – too long we have tarried.

But what shall we do for a ring?"

They sailed away...

...for a year and a day...

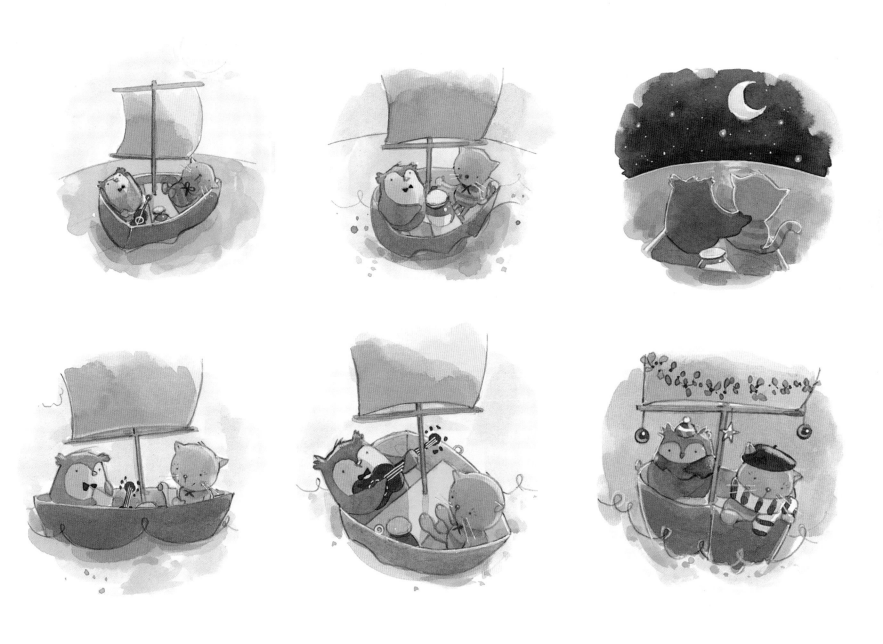

...to the land where the Bong-tree grows.

And there in a wood a **Piggy-wig** stood,
with a ring at the end of his nose,
his nose, his nose,

with a ring at the
end of his nose.

''Dear Pig, are you willing

to sell for one shilling, your ring?"

Said the Piggy, "I will!"

So they took it away,

and were married
next day,

by the Turkey who
lives on the hill.

They dined on mince, and slices of quince,

which they ate with a runcible spoon.

And hand in hand, on the edge of the sand,
they danced by the light of the moon,

the moon, the moon,
they danced by the light of the moon.

Designed by Caroline Spatz
Editor: Lesley Sims

This edition first published in 2012 by Usborne Publishing Ltd., Usborne House,
83-85 Saffron Hill, London EC1N 8RT, England. www.usborne.com
Copyright © 2012, 2010 Usborne Publishing Ltd.